Amy and the Feelings Basket

Brave Beats the Bullies

By Debbie K

Illustrated by Louise Grundy

Amy and the Feelings Basket
Brave Beats the Bullies

Ashbridge Publishing

P.O. Box 4227, Bracknell. RG42 9PW

First Published in 2013 by Ashbridge Publishing

ISBN 978-0-9926654-2-5

All characters are fictional.
Any similarity to any actual person is purely coincidental.

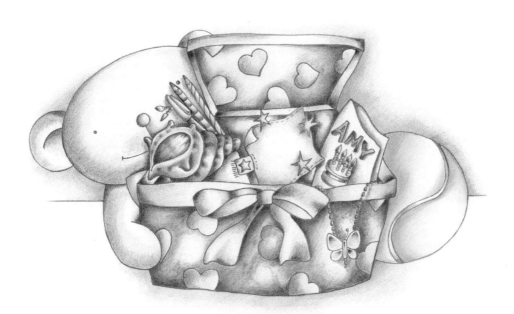

This is Amy

She lives in England with her
mum and dad, Mr and Mrs Thorpe.

A little while ago, Amy's mum gave her
a very special present - a feelings basket.
It's the magical place where Amy's
feelings live until she needs them...

It was a bright, sunny morning and Amy was feeling very excited. It was the day her class were allowed to take one of their toys into school to show the other children.

Thomas, her favourite teddy, looked up at her hopefully.
"Not today, Thomas," she said, patting him softly on the head. "Today, I'm going to take my tree house."

The tree house was a present from Amy's mum. It had belonged to Mrs Thorpe when she was a little girl and Amy loved playing with it. The top was round and green, like a tree full of leaves, and when you pressed hard on the top, it popped open. There was a bedroom, a living room and a kitchen all hidden inside. The tree people were inside too. There was a whole family and a dog.
"One, two, three, four, five," Amy counted as she pushed each member of the family down the slide to the car waiting at the bottom.
"It would be great if there was a slide outside our bedroom window," Amy suggested to Thomas. "We could slide into the garden every morning."

Amy placed the tree people back in the living room and pushed hard on the top. It closed with a loud "click". She picked up the tree house, gave Thomas a goodbye hug and skipped out of her bedroom and off to school.

After first playtime, Miss Watson, the teacher, told all the children that they could take out their toys to show each other. Amy looked around her table to see what the other children had brought with them. Yin had a Lego tank. Beth had a Barbie fashion doll. Liam showed off his dinosaur that turned into a car. Mia had a Build a Bear called Josie. Jacob stood up and showed everyone how his jet plane could swoop through the sky. Amy was last to show her toy. She carefully got it out of the bag and placed it up on the table.

"This is my tree house," she said with pride, pressing hard on the top of the tree. It popped open to show the rooms inside.

"I've never seen one of those before," said Beth. "Was it for Christmas?"

"No," replied Amy. "My mum gave it to me. It was hers when she was a little girl."

Yin, Mia and Jacob started laughing too.
Amy was a little confused why they were laughing at
her. They obviously didn't realise how much fun the
tree house could be.

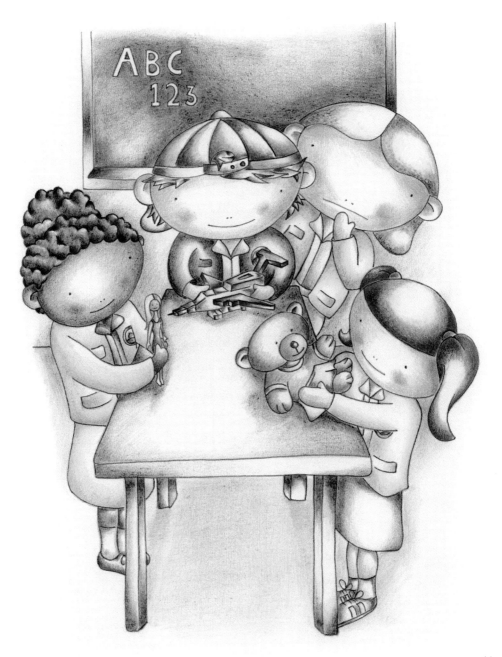

"Look what it can do," said Amy as she picked up the daddy figure and placed him at the top of the slide. She gave him a nudge and smiled as he glided down the slide onto their desk.

"Wow, a slide, I've never seen one of those before," said Jacob, sounding mean.

Amy thought about what the other children had. Some of them had things that could move. Maybe they would like it more if they saw the car. She pulled it out of the garage and placed each of the characters inside, driving it with a "brum brum" across the desk.
Liam looked up at her. "You're such a baby with your baby toys."
"Yeah, you and your baby toys," Jacob echoed laughing at her.

Amy looked at Mia and Beth. Mia was laughing along with the boys but Beth just looked down at her doll.
"Do you want to play with my tree house?" Amy asked Beth eagerly.
Beth just shook her head, trying not to look up.
Amy didn't know what to do. She could feel her cheeks growing hot and tears were pricking at the corner of her eyes.

"Are you going to cry like a baby now?" Liam teased.

Amy did everything she could to stop the tears but they started to fall down her cheeks. She didn't understand why they were all laughing at her. She grabbed the tree house from the table and put it back in her bag. She hated the tree house now too. All the other children played with their toys while Amy sat alone until Miss Watson told everyone it was lunchtime. Amy turned hopefully to Beth. "Shall we play with your doll in the playground?"

"Yes, go and play with the baby," snarled Liam. Beth shook her head. "I don't want to play with her, she's a baby," she said.

Even Beth, her best friend, was calling her a baby now. She grabbed her lunchbox and went and sat in the corner, far away from all the other children. As she ate her sandwiches, she wished and wished she had her feelings basket with her. She really didn't understand why the others were being mean and she felt so lonely.

When Amy got home, she ran straight up the stairs into her bedroom. She reached under the bed and pulled out her special piece of material. Placing it on top of the bed, she pulled hard on the corner and the magic basket popped into life.

Amy peeped in and was happy to see one of her feelings already waiting, waving up at her. He jumped on to her hand as she dipped it into the basket and held on tightly to her thumb. She felt the magic start to work. It tingled from the tips of her fingers all the way up to the top of her head.

This feeling was a silver colour, a little like the shiny parts of Amy's bike. He was round like a pebble and he sat with his legs pulled up in front of him, hugging his knees. Amy knew straight away that this feeling was Lonely.

Lonely looked up at Amy through his long eyelashes. "Hi," he said very quietly.

"Hello," said Amy, placing him onto the bed.

"Please can I have a hug?" he said, stretching his arms up high in the air. Amy wrapped her arms around him and gave him a big hug. She noticed that Lonely didn't feel as hard as he looked. She thought he was made of metal, but actually he was very soft and lovely to hug.

"That has made me feel a little better already," said Amy with a sigh.

Lonely agreed. "So, what has made you feel so lonely today?" he asked.

Amy told him about everything that had happened at school. How excited she had been to show the others her tree house. How they had laughed at it for being old and a baby toy. She also explained that Beth had not wanted to spend time with her at lunchtime.

"I felt so alone," Amy cried. "I can't understand why Beth won't talk to me either."

Lonely looked up at Amy. "I think sometimes people don't always do the right thing because they are scared of what others will think of them. Maybe Beth wanted to help you but was scared that Liam would be nasty to her if she did."

"But she wouldn't even look at me when I asked her to play."

"She probably felt embarrassed that she couldn't help you. Looking at you might have made her feel even worse," suggested Lonely.
 "Hmm, I guess," said Amy deep in thought. "Do you think Beth still wants to be my friend?"

"Yes, of course," Lonely replied. "I expect that while the boys were picking on you, she wanted to keep out of the way. I'm sure she'll be happy to play with you again tomorrow. Liam and Jacob will probably have forgotten all about it by then too."

Amy let out a big sigh. She felt much better
knowing that Beth would talk to her tomorrow and
that the boys would not call her names.
"Do you feel a little less lonely now?" asked Lonely.
 "Yes, thank you," she smiled.

They sat together for a while enjoying each other's company before Amy thanked Lonely for spending time with her. She gently placed him back in the basket, closed it and lay the sparkly blue piece of material in her safe place under the bed.

The next morning Amy got ready for school, feeling much more cheerful after her chat with Lonely. She ran through the school gates looking for Beth. Liam and Jacob jumped out from behind the climbing frame.

"Good morning, cry baby," they both said in a sing-song voice.
Amy stopped in front of them.

 "We've got a present for you, little baby," said Liam, laughing. As he said it, he threw a baby rattle hard at Amy.
"Ow," Amy cried as it hit her leg.
"What are you going to do, little baby, run to the teacher and cry?" Liam taunted as he picked up the rattle and threw it again. This time the rattle hit Amy on the arm and it really hurt. She couldn't help the tears from spilling out.
"Just leave me alone," she cried.
"Cry baby, cry baby," Liam and Jacob shouted as they ran into the classroom.
Amy quickly wiped the tears from her eyes.

She didn't want Miss Watson to know the boys had hurt her. She was worried that if she told, it would just make the boys pick on her even more and maybe she would get into trouble for telling tales. In fact Amy didn't tell anyone, even though Liam and Jacob made mean comments all day long.

To make things worse, Beth still didn't want to play with her. Nobody wanted to play with her. By the end of the day, Amy believed that the boys were right and that she was a baby. She thought that no-one would ever want to play with her again.

When she arrived home Amy thought about telling her mum, but something was stopping her from doing it and she didn't know what it was. She ran up the stairs as fast as her legs would carry her to talk to her feelings and see if they could help her again. Although she still felt very lonely, there was another feeling inside too, it made her cheeks go hot every time she thought about what had happened at school. Amy quickly opened up the magic basket and looked inside. No-one was waiting for her.

"Please help me," Amy whispered. "I need to talk to someone and I don't know what to do."
After a few seconds, one feeling was pushed into

the middle by the others. He looked like he really didn't want to be there. Amy knew she needed to be very gentle with this feeling.

As the magic began to work and the feeling grew bigger Amy could see that this feeling was pale pink and had bright red cheeks, making it look like his cheeks were on fire. As she looked closer she could see that the feeling was smooth, with soft little hairs all over his body. His fur reminded Amy of her velvet teddy, Sugarlump. She also noticed that this feeling had his hands over his eyes, as if he was trying to hide. He was still covering his eyes, even when he got to the top of the basket. She carefully placed him on the bed and moved the basket to one side.

Amy realised she would have to introduce herself first. "Hello. I'm Amy, who are you?"

"I'm Ashamed," said the feeling very quietly.

"I'm not sure I know what ashamed is," said Amy as she peered closer, trying to get him to look at her.

"Ashamed is what you feel when you think you have done something wrong," said the feeling.

"You're right. I do feel that I've done something wrong." Amy flopped down onto the bed. "I must have done something really silly for the boys to pick on me like this. Beth still won't talk to me either. I don't know what to do. I can't tell anyone about it."

Amy looked over at Ashamed, who peeped out a little from under his hands.

"You have nothing to feel ashamed about," he said quietly. "You didn't do anything to make the boys cross with you. You couldn't help but cry when they laughed at you and hurt you. They're just being bullies."

"But how do I get them to stop?" Amy asked. "Yesterday, Lonely thought that they would forget about picking on me, but they haven't. Today has been even worse and I don't want it to be the same tomorrow and the next day."

"I think you need to speak to mum," suggested Ashamed.

"But mum might be cross that I've been a baby, or she might tell Miss Watson which will make them bully me even more."

"It's best to tell a grown up when you're being bullied as they know how to sort it out. You don't need to feel ashamed about it." As Ashamed said this, he took away one of the hands coving his eyes and gave Amy's thumb a little squeeze. "I'll come with you if you like?"
"Yes, I would like that," replied Amy. Having Ashamed by her side might help her find the right words to say.

Together, they went downstairs and told mum everything that had happened. Mum didn't get cross at all and she understood why Amy had felt lonely and ashamed. She explained that these were very normal feelings to have when you're being bullied.

She went on to say, "People can be bullies when they don't feel confident about themselves. It's usually when something has happened to make them feel scared, nervous or lonely. You see, Liam has a new baby sister and his mum says that he's having a bit of trouble welcoming her into the family."

"But why is he being mean to me and not his sister?" asked Amy.

"Liam's mum and dad need to look after his little sister a lot at the moment, so I think he feels a bit left out. If he doesn't feel important at home, then he will try to make himself feel more important at school. The one way Liam has worked out how to do this is by bullying you. He thinks it will make him feel better. The other children are following his lead because they are too scared not to."

"So what do I do?" asked Amy. "It's not my fault he has a new sister and he's not happy."

"I know, it's not your fault and it's not fair what Liam is doing, but we need to help him."

"Help him?" asked Amy, feeling very shocked.

"Yes, we help him remember that you're not a baby and he shouldn't treat you like one. If you tell him that you're not a baby and you don't care what he calls you then he can't keep picking on you."

"I don't think I can do it. It really hurts my feelings when he calls me a baby."

Mum thought for a moment. "Does it really matter what he calls you? You know you're not a baby. The other children in the class know you're not a baby too. If you're confident about who you are then it doesn't matter what anyone else calls you, does it?"

"I guess not," replied Amy looking at her feet.

"You don't sound very sure," said mum. "Are you
sure you're not a baby?" she asked as she pulled
Amy onto her knee to tickle her.

"No, I'm not a baby," Amy giggled.
"Tell me again, louder,"
"I'm not a baby," said Amy a little louder.
"Much louder," said mum as she dropped Amy onto
the sofa and stood up like a soldier.
"I am not a baby," shouted Amy copying mum and
standing tall like a soldier too.

"It takes a brave soldier to stand up to a bully and
not let them hurt you."
"I can do it," said Amy.
"I know you can," said mum. "If Liam does continue
to pick on you, you must tell Miss Watson. She can
help you by explaining to Liam how you feel and how
he should behave. Telling your teacher is not going
to get you into trouble."

"Okay, I'd like to be brave and tell him myself first,
though," said Amy.
"Great idea," said mum as she planted a wet kiss on
Amy's cheek. Ashamed peeped out from under his
hands and smiled.

The next morning, once Amy was ready for school, she took out her feelings basket and looked inside.

"Excuse me," said Amy politely, "is it possible for Brave to come with me to school today? I think I need some extra help."
There was a lot of commotion in the basket, and then all of a sudden one of the feelings waved up at Amy from the middle.

Amy scooped the feeling from the basket. As she drew out her hand she looked into the face of a very red, square feeling. He leapt to his feet waving around a sword and shield, which looked much too big for him.

"Wow, are you Brave?" asked Amy.
"Yes, I am," said Brave. "I'm going to save you from the bullies."

"But fighting isn't going to get us anywhere. Mum said we have to be confident and brave with our words."

"Oh," said Brave, a little disappointed. He dropped the sword and shield to his side. "I guess I can help with that too."

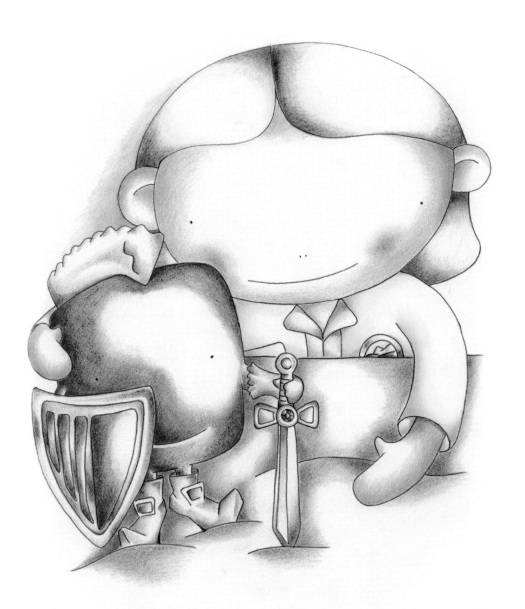

"Great," said Amy. "You can help me feel brave all
day." Before Brave knew what was happening Amy
had said the magic words "pocket size" and he was
shrinking again. Amy popped Brave into her pocket.

At school Amy found Beth in the playground. She
bravely told Beth that she had felt lonely over the
last two days without her to play with.

"I understand that you didn't want Liam to pick on you too," explained Amy. "But we both need to be brave together. I'm going to talk to him, will you come with me?"

"I'm not sure I feel as brave as you but I will come with you," said Beth. "I'm really sorry for not helping you before. Can we still be friends?"

"Of course," said Amy with a smile.
Amy rested her hand in her pocket and felt Brave grab her finger. He gave it a little squeeze. She felt the tingly brave feeling run up her finger, into her hand, all the way up her arm and into her body. She felt brave right down to the tips of her toes.

Liam and Jacob were in the corner of the playground, playing football.
"Here comes the baby and her baby friend," Liam said as Amy and Beth got closer.

"I'm not a baby," Amy replied. "You can call me baby as much as you want but I know it's not true."

Liam looked shocked. "Okay, whatever you say, baby," he replied.

"Come on Beth," said Amy as she bravely turned

and walked away from Liam. "Let's go and play over the other side of the playground."

For once Liam didn't have anything to say. He kicked the football hard against the wall and pretended to Jacob that he didn't care.

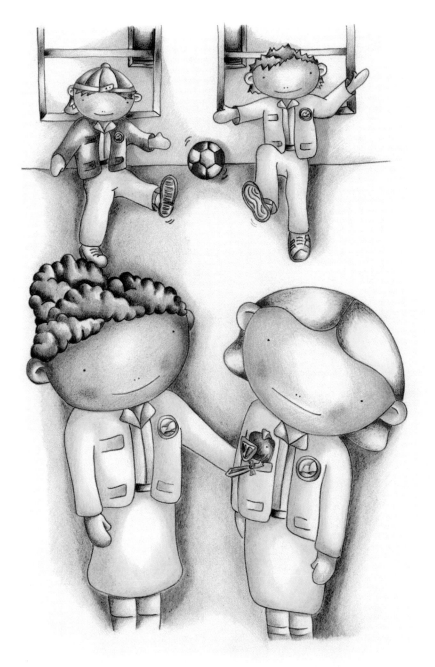

Amy wasn't sure if Liam would say something nasty to her later but she knew that if she stayed brave then Liam's words couldn't hurt her any more.

Amy and Beth walked across the playground together, feeling much happier that they were friends again. Amy peeped into her pocket and Brave smiled up at her with a very proud look on his face. Amy was finally looking forward to a fun day at school.

My feelings

Have you ever felt lonely? Did you do something to stop feeling lonely or did you wait for someone to come and keep you company?

Have you ever seen any of your friends get bullied? If you did, did you act like Jacob or Beth or did you do something different?

Have you ever been bullied by someone? Do you know why they bullied you? How did it make you feel? Were you able to stop the bully?

If you were being bullied, who would you tell:
- Your mum or dad?
- Your teacher?
- Your friend?
- Someone else?

Stand up tall and think how you would feel if Brave was in your pocket. What would you say to a bully?

There are some blank pages at the back of this book for you to write down your answers or draw some fun feelings pictures.

Other books in the Amy and the Feelings Basket series:

The Magic Basket

Join Amy in exploring her feelings basket for the first time, meeting Curious and Sad on this very special journey.

Starting School - Confidence Leads the Way

It's the last day of the summer holiday. Tomorrow Amy starts her new school. Join Amy as her feelings help her prepare for the big day.

The New Arrival Love Lends a Hand

Amy's baby brother has finally arrived. After the long wait, Amy thought she would feel happy but a few other feelings get in the way.

For more information on Amy and her Feelings Basket visit: www.feelingsbasket.co.uk

Printed in Great Britain
by Amazon.co.uk, Ltd.,
Marston Gate.